Calling All Pets!

Don't miss any of the *paw*fectly fun
books in the **PET HOTEL** series!

PET HOTEL

Calling All Pets!

by Kate Finch

illustrated by
John Steven Gurney

SCHOLASTIC INC.

Special thanks to Jane Clarke

For Andrew and Robert, whose pets turned our house into a pet hotel.

No part of this work may be reproduced, stored in a retrieval system, or transmitted in any form or by any means, electronic, mechanical, photocopying, recording, or otherwise, without written permission of the publisher. For information regarding permission, write to Working Partners Limited, Stanley House, St. Chad's Place, London WC1X 9HH, United Kingdom.

ISBN 978-0-545-50180-4

12 11 10 9 8 7 6 5 4 3 2 1   13 14 15 16 17 18/0

Printed in the U.S.A.   40
First printing, July 2013

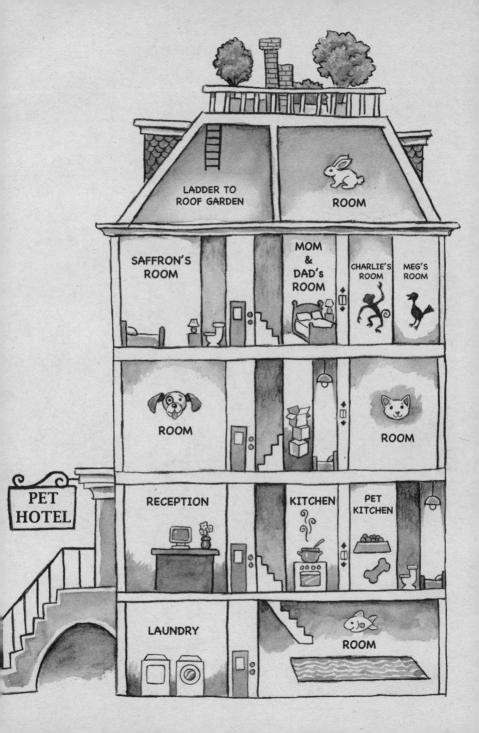

CHAPTER 1

WELCOME TO GAZEBO SQUARE!

Eight-year-old twins Charlie and Meg beamed as they read the sign. The street was bustling with brightly colored tents and happy, smiling people.

"I can't believe we're really going to live here!" Charlie exclaimed, hoisting up his heavy backpack.

Meg sniffed the air. "Yum!" she murmured. "Chocolate and spices and flowers . . ."

Dad heaved an enormous suitcase down the last step from the train station and paused to catch his breath. "This is a very special place," he said with a grin. "The farmers' market is open every day. Gazebo Square makes everyone feel at home."

"You're going to love Great-Great-Aunt Saffron's hotel!" Mom added.

"I hope we love Great-Great-Aunt Saffron," Charlie whispered to Meg. "She must be very, very old."

Meg nodded. Mom and Dad were going to run the hotel so their great-great-aunt didn't have to move to a retirement home.

"Follow me!" Mom called over her shoulder. They set off through the rainbow maze of tents. There were fruit and vegetable stands, cheese and milk stands, even a cupcake stand! The twins gazed around in eye-popping wonder. Gazebo Square was awfully different from their old home in the country!

Mom paused by a circular, open-air hut where a band was playing cheerful calypso music on steel drums.

"This is the gazebo the square was named after," she announced.

"Cool!" Meg and Charlie said together.

"See the old archway that the workmen are fixing?" Mom said, pointing to the nearby entrance to the square. "That leads to a park with trees and a pond!"

"Are there any animals there?" Charlie asked hopefully. "I haven't seen any yet. . . ."

But before Mom could answer, a bundle of yellow fur raced out from under a tent. It was heading straight for them! Meg dropped her heavy bag in surprise.

It was a golden retriever puppy. He had soft, floppy ears, a damp nose, and a wagging tail. He held a bone-shaped cookie in his mouth, but only for a second. Then the puppy gobbled it up, licked his lips, and gazed at Charlie and Meg with big, dark eyes.

"Paco!" a deep voice called.

The twins looked up. The voice belonged to a tall man with thick, curly hair. He wore a red-and-green T-shirt with *Hecho en Mexico* on the front.

"*Lo siento*, sorry . . ." The man handed Meg her bag and grabbed Paco's trailing leash. "He's been raiding the Pet Bakery on Park Street again! My little puppy's a big handful," he told them with a friendly grin.

"Paco's very cute!" Meg said, tickling the puppy under his furry chin. "I love dogs."

Charlie stroked Paco's back. "I wish we had a cat!" he sighed. Paco pricked up his ears and wagged his tail. "Or a puppy," Charlie added with a laugh.

The man looked at the family's luggage. "Moving in?" he asked.

"Yes, to Diamond Hotel," Mom told him.

"Welcome, neighbors!" the man exclaimed. "I run Cocina Mexicana." He pointed to his stall. "My name's Juan. Come and see me when you're hungry!"

They promised that they would, and waved good-bye. As they walked along Gazebo Square, Charlie daydreamed about their new home.

"Diamond Hotel," he murmured. "It sounds like somewhere movie stars would stay."

"It might be like a palace!" Meg whispered to her brother, eyes shining.

Mom had stopped in front of a tall brownstone. It was covered in crumbly plaster that might once have been brown but now looked almost black. Over the battered door was a wooden sign that read THE DIAMOND HOTEL.

The twins' mouths dropped open.

"It's called that because Diamond is Saffron's last name," Mom explained, raising her voice as one of the workmen at the archway nearby turned on a big drill. The vibrations made the ground rumble. Bits of plaster fell off the front of Diamond Hotel and dust showered down on the twins' heads.

Plunk! The hotel sign landed with a *thud* at their feet.

Meg and Charlie looked at each other. What would Diamond Hotel be like inside?

Dad rapped on the rickety wooden door, but there was no answer.

"Maybe it's unlocked." Meg turned the handle, and the door slowly creaked open.

The twins stepped into a dim hall jam-packed with boxes, coats, shoes, and umbrellas. Everything was covered in a thick layer of dust. It rose in a cloud as they dropped their luggage on the moth-eaten carpet.

Mom took one look inside and clapped her hand to her mouth.

Dad flicked a light switch.

"Not working," he said, coughing.

"Aunt Saffron," Mom called. "We're here!"

There was no reply. Where could Aunt Saffron be?

CHAPTER 2

Dad picked his way across the room to the front desk. "There's a reservation book," he murmured. Charlie and Meg crowded around as Dad brushed off the dust. The open pages were blank, except for the name of one guest. . . .

"Mrs. Ponsonby," they read together.

"That's today's date!" Dad exclaimed. "It looks like she's due to arrive any minute."

Just then, there was a knock on the door.

Meg rushed to open it. Standing on the doorstep was a woman in a bright-pink suit. By her side, on a leash, was a tiny poodle with a glittery silver collar.

As Meg opened her mouth to greet them, Mrs. Ponsonby stepped past her into the hall. "Dear me!" she said, looking around in disgust.

Her poodle trotted after her and snuffled at the coat stand. It wagged its tail.

"This is a run-down dump!" the woman declared. "We can't spend the night in a place like this. Come on, Petal! We're leaving!"

She swept out, dragging the curious poodle behind her.

"I think Petal wanted to stay!" Charlie snickered.

Mom was looking worried. "How will we keep this place going if we don't have any guests?" she said under her breath. "And where in the world is Saffron?"

"The hotel has five floors. We need a search party," Dad said.

"That's us!" Charlie declared. "We'll start at the bottom and work our way up."

Meg and Charlie clattered down the stairs

behind the reception desk. The basement shimmered with a misty green glow. Light from the window filtered through the rubbery leaves of a huge plant. It was growing beside an old swimming pool full of water lilies.

"Wow!" Meg gasped.

"There are fish in there!" Charlie pointed out a big orange goldfish hiding beneath a lily pad. "Awesome!"

The twins raced back upstairs. Mom and Dad were still complaining about the dust.

"This place has a pond!" Charlie yelled to them. He grinned at Meg. "Let's see what else there is."

They dashed in and out of the rambling rooms. On the second floor was a room that had huge palm trees on the wallpaper and statues of pharaohs by the fireplace. On the windowsill was a carved black cat wearing a golden necklace.

"It's like being in ancient Egypt!" Meg cried.

On the third floor was a sky-blue bedroom with sunshine-yellow curtains. Brightly colored birds were painted on the walls.

"I'd love for this to be my room," Meg

sighed, gazing at a beautiful blue parrot with a ruby-red tail.

Right next door was a room with a leopard-print carpet, and paintings of wild animals on the walls.

"Whoa," Charlie said, pointing to a picture of an elephant. "I'd choose this room —"

He stopped. Meg had her finger on her lips and was pointing to the next flight of stairs.

Above them, something was making a cooing noise.

They climbed up to the attic. A little iron ladder was fixed to the wall near the top of the staircase, with a ceiling hatch above it. Charlie scrambled up and pushed the hatch open. He was so high up, he could see all of Gazebo Square.

"It's a roof garden!" he announced.

Meg clambered out behind him. The flat roof was packed with pots of bright flowers, bushes, and small trees. A very old woman with long silver hair was holding out a handful of seeds to a cooing pigeon. She was wearing baggy bell-bottomed pants and a bright orange-and-purple blouse with long sleeves that billowed in the breeze.

"Great-Great-Aunt Saffron!" the twins declared together.

"Call me Saffron, my dears!" Saffron's long earrings jangled as she threw her turquoise feather boa around her wrinkly neck. She gave the twins a huge smile that lit up her face. "I had completely forgotten that you were coming," she admitted. "But

I'm very happy you're here. I haven't seen you since you were babies."

"It's good to see you, too," Meg told her. "I like the bells on your earrings and the feathers on your boa!"

"Thank you," Saffron said. "I like your bird earrings, Meg. And your tiger T-shirt, Charlie. You must be fond of animals, like I am."

"We are!" the twins exclaimed.

"Mom and Dad will be glad we found you," Charlie said.

"They're worried because Mrs. Ponsonby and her poodle refused to stay," Meg explained.

"Things have a way of working themselves out," Saffron said with a smile. "Let's go and get something to eat." She carefully led the way down the ladder and pulled open a hidden door in the wall.

"You have an elevator?" Charlie exclaimed.

"Yes, dear, and a dumbwaiter, too — that's a little elevator to bring food and things up from the kitchen," Saffron told them. Once they stepped inside, the elevator thunked and clattered down to the reception level.

Meg and Charlie grinned at each other. Living at Diamond Hotel was already an adventure!

CHAPTER 3

"I've looked in the kitchen, and all I can find to eat is a loaf of bread with a piece nibbled out of it," Mom announced after she'd given Saffron a big hug hello. "I think there must be a mouse!"

"We'll have to put down a humane trap," Dad said.

"We all have to eat, my dears," Saffron remarked. She took a turquoise wallet out of her pocket and tipped some money into Charlie's hands. "Why don't you two go get something from Cocina Mexicana?" she told the twins.

Meg and Charlie raced outside.

"We get to see Paco again," said Charlie with a grin. But when they reached Juan's stall, the puppy wasn't there.

"Paco ran off again!" Juan explained with a sigh. "But I'm sure he'll be back soon. Now, how can I help my new neighbors?"

"Dinner for five, please!" Charlie held out a handful of bills.

"No problem. You'll love my chicken mole with rice and beans!" Juan began to box up the delicious spicy food. Suddenly, the drilling started up again nearby. Juan jumped, dropping a piece of chicken onto the ground. A shower of gritty dust fell onto Cocina Mexicana's stripy tent.

"I'd better clean that off before it gets in the food." Juan took a brush and pan and stood on an overturned vegetable crate so he could reach the top of the tent.

Out of the corner of her eye, Meg spotted Paco hurtling toward them.

"Your puppy's coming back!" she exclaimed in delight.

As Paco ran, his big eyes were fixed on the piece of chicken Juan had dropped.

"He's not watching where he's going!" shouted Charlie. "Look out!"

But it was too late. Paco smashed into the crate Juan was standing on.

Crash!

"Ow!" Juan yelled as he fell to the ground.

He rolled up the right leg of his jeans. The twins gazed in horror at Juan's swollen ankle. Paco's ears and tail drooped.

Meg turned to the woman at Carmen's Cupcake Collection, the tent next to Cocina Mexicana.

"Please — call an ambulance!" she cried. "Juan hurt his ankle!"

"Don't worry," Charlie reassured Juan. "They'll take care of everything at the hospital."

"But Paco has nowhere to stay," Juan murmured, wincing as he tried to move his leg. "Who will look after him?"

Meg and Charlie glanced at each other. Together, they said, "We will!"

Juan gave a sigh of relief. "Thanks," he said. "I know he'll love staying with you."

The ambulance arrived in a whir of red-and-white lights. The crew hurried over with a stretcher and helped Juan into the back of the ambulance.

"Paco's leash and dog food are in a back-pack under the stall," Juan called.

"Got it!" Charlie replied.

The ambulance crew slammed the doors shut. Paco whimpered as they sped off.

"Don't worry. Juan will be back soon," Meg told him. She scooped up the little puppy.

Charlie patted Paco's head, and the end of the puppy's tail twitched. "You'll be okay with us, Paco," he said. "Let's go back to Diamond Hotel."

"Of course Paco can stay here until Juan's better!" Saffron declared the instant she heard what had happened. Mom and Dad nodded.

"We could turn one of the hotel rooms into a bedroom for him," Meg suggested.

Mom took Juan's bag from Charlie. "Go and help Paco settle in. I'll keep our dinner warm," she told the twins.

Saffron's knees were too stiff for her to take the stairs, so they followed her into the elevator. The bells on her earrings chimed as she pushed the button that said "2." She winked at the twins.

"I know *exactly* the right room for Paco," Saffron said.

When they reached the second floor, the twins followed her down the hall to the end furthest from the Egyptian room. Saffron opened a door, and they stepped into another large room. The wallpaper was patterned with leafy oak trees, and the moth-eaten carpet looked like autumn leaves.

"It's like a forest in here!" Charlie laughed.

Meg put Paco down. The puppy scampered around the room, wagging his tail. He stopped by the blocked-off fireplace and sniffed curiously. Meg brushed away the dust.

"The tiles have cute little woodland creatures on them," she said in delight. "I can see a baby squirrel, a rabbit —"

Paco's ears pricked up.

"Woof!" His plump little body wiggled so wildly that he caught sight of the end of his own tail. *"Woof, woof, woof!"* Paco chased after it, racing around and around in a circle.

The twins and Saffron giggled.

"That's your tail, Paco, not a rabbit," Charlie said.

All of a sudden, Paco gave an enormous yawn and lay down with his head on his big puppy paws.

"Puppies need lots of naps," Meg remarked.

"So do I!" Saffron yawned so hard that her earrings jangled.

"We'll keep an eye on Paco," Charlie told her. "You go and rest."

Half an hour later, Paco was snuggled up in a comfy bed made of old towels. Next to

the snoozing puppy, the twins had put out
cereal bowls full of puppy food and water.
Meg tiptoed to the fireplace and laid Paco's
leash on the mantle.

"It looks like a puppy hotel room!"
Charlie joked as they carefully closed the
door and went down to join Mom, Dad, and
Saffron for Juan's delicious dinner.

CHAPTER 4

"Now, my dears, we must take Paco for a little walk," Saffron informed them after they'd finished eating. She rummaged in Juan's backpack and pulled out some small plastic bags. "We can use these to clean up after him," she explained.

Meg rushed off to fetch Paco and his leash.

"He ate his whole dinner," she announced when she returned.

Paco yapped excitedly as the twins and Saffron took him outside. Gazebo Square was quieter now that the stalls had been packed up and the construction workers had gone home. Juan's empty stall had a note stuck to it. Charlie read it aloud:

Your things are safe with me.
Get well soon. Love, Carmen.

"Such good neighbors!" Saffron smiled, throwing her turquoise feather boa around her neck.

They passed a pharmacy and a clothing store. Outside the bookstore was a low table with a pile of books on it. A woman in a stripy dress was arranging them into a display.

"Bianca!" Saffron called to the woman. "Meet Meg and Charlie, my great-great-niece and nephew!"

Bianca turned and grinned at them. "Welcome to Bianca's Books! We have lots of stories for kids here." Paco barked. "And some books about puppies, too," she added with a laugh.

The twins looked through the pile of books while Saffron chatted with Bianca.

After a few minutes, Saffron called the twins over.

"Bianca has some wonderful news," Saffron told them. "Her sister just had a baby."

"That's so nice!" said Meg. "Have you met the baby yet?"

Bianca shook her head. "Not yet — they live far away, and I can't leave Bouncer by herself. She's my pet rabbit," she explained.

Saffron winked at the twins. Charlie and Meg shared a grin.

"We'll take care of Bouncer so you can go!" Charlie said. "We're already looking after Paco."

Bianca's eyes lit up. "Really? That's so nice of you!"

They arranged for Bianca to bring Bouncer to Diamond Hotel the next day. Waving good-bye, they made their way through the square. Paco tugged them through the archway that led into the park. Saffron walked with tiny, careful steps, and her silver hair billowed in the warm breeze. Charlie linked his arm with hers.

"Thank you, dear." Saffron sat down on a park bench and loosened her boa. It flopped onto the bench.

Paco's ears pricked up.

"Grrr!" The puppy growled playfully, tugging at the end of the boa. He wrestled it off the bench and rolled around. Soon only his nose and tail stuck out from the pile of turquoise feathers.

"Paco's a dog-bird!" Meg giggled.

"I've had that boa since the 1960s," Saffron said, "but I've never had as much fun with it as Paco is!"

"I'll rescue it." Charlie plucked the slobbery boa from Paco's jaws and held it above his head.

"Yip! Yip! Yip!" Paco sprang up and down, trying to snatch an end. At last, he gave a big sigh and lay down, panting.

"He's worn out again," Saffron said with a smile. Charlie passed her the boa.

Meg picked up the exhausted puppy, and they walked back to the hotel. She laid Paco in his towel bed.

"Night night, sleep tight," Meg whispered.

In an instant, the room was filled with the gentle rumble of puppy snores.

>< >< ><

The next morning, when Charlie opened his eyes, excitement bubbled up inside him. He was in his amazing new jungle bedroom in Diamond Hotel, *and* he and Meg were looking after Juan's puppy!

"Woof!" He could hear Paco barking on the floor below.

"Paco's up!" Meg called from her room.

Charlie leaped out of bed and pulled on his paw-print robe. Meg was already waiting for him in the hallway in her pajamas. They ran down to the forest room and opened the door.

Before they could blink, a yellow blur of fur shot between their legs and scampered down the staircase. Paco! The twins raced after him. Luckily, Dad was coming up the stairs and scooped up the little puppy.

"I think someone needs to go out," Dad said. "Don't you, Paco?"

While Dad took Paco to the park, the twins showered and dressed, then helped Mom and Saffron get breakfast ready. Soon, a stack of blueberry pancakes was giving off a delicious scent.

"Smells good!" said Dad, when he came back in with Paco. The little puppy barked at the pancakes.

"Paco wants his breakfast, too," Meg said. She grabbed a bowl and poured out some puppy food. While the family sat down to eat the pancakes, Paco happily chomped on his breakfast nearby.

As Charlie was finishing off the last blueberry pancake, the doorbell rang.

Meg and Charlie grinned. "That must be Bianca and Bouncer," said Meg. "Now we have a rabbit staying at Diamond Hotel!"

CHAPTER 5

The twins ran to the hall to answer the door. Bianca was standing on the front step, holding a wicker basket with a tiny door on the front. Through the gaps, Meg and Charlie could see a small gray rabbit with floppy ears.

"I'm so glad you can take care of her while I'm gone," Bianca said. In her other hand was a bag, which she passed to Charlie. "Bouncer's grooming brushes and food are in here — and some books for you both, as a special thank-you."

"Thanks!" said Charlie and Meg together.

Bouncer snuffled, wiggling her long whiskers.

"She's so cute," said Meg. "We'll be sure to take good care of her."

Saffron and the twins took Bouncer up to the old playroom in the attic. They turned the playpen into a rabbit run, and Meg laid a toy box on its side to make a cozy bed. She arranged an old towel inside of it for Bouncer to sleep on.

"The flowery wallpaper makes this room look like a meadow," said Meg. "It's perfect for a rabbit!"

Gently, Meg took Bouncer out of her travel basket. The bunny was even smaller and lighter than Paco, with silky, soft fur.

"As long as we keep the door closed, Bouncer can run around the room," said Saffron. "We'll put her in her run when she's by herself."

Meg placed Bouncer on the carpet. She wiggled her nose, then lolloped over to an old doll's house and snuffled at the tiny windows.

Charlie was looking through one of the books Bianca had given them. He showed it to Meg and Saffron. "Look — it's called *Pet Expert*."

"You can learn more about Paco and Bouncer," Saffron said. "Now, my dears, I'm going to get us all some lemonade."

She went out to the landing and the twins heard the *ping* of the elevator doors opening. Together, they laid *Pet Expert* on the carpet and flipped through the pages.

Between the twins appeared a shiny black nose.

"Paco!" said Meg with a gasp. "How did you get in?"

Paco barked and wagged his tail.

Charlie stared at Meg. "Saffron must have forgotten to shut the door. If Paco can get in — Bouncer can get out!"

The twins jumped up. The tip of Bouncer's tail was just disappearing through the door.

"We have to catch her!" Meg said.

Bouncer hopped out onto the landing just as the elevator arrived. *Ping!* The doors opened to reveal Saffron, holding a tray of glasses filled with sparkling lemonade. "Who's thirsty?" she asked.

As she stepped out of the elevator, Bouncer jumped inside.

"Stop that elevator!" shouted Charlie.

Saffron's eyes widened as she spotted Bouncer. "Oh, dear . . ."

Meg and Charlie lunged toward the elevator, but they were too late. The doors closed and the elevator clunked back down — taking Bouncer with it!

"The elevator automatically goes back to the ground floor," Saffron said quickly. "Hurry — maybe you can catch up with it!"

The twins ran down the stairs.

"Poor Bouncer," Charlie said. "She'll be so scared!"

They ran across the landing on the bedroom floor, then down the next set of stairs to the floor with the forest room. Meg could feel her heart pounding. Paco was running beside them, his pink tongue hanging out.

A few moments later, they reached the ground floor. But the elevator doors were already open.

"Oh, no," Charlie said. "We're too late. Where's Bouncer?"

Meg peered under the reception desk while Charlie checked the kitchen next door. "Any sign of her?" she asked. Charlie shook his head.

Paco was sniffing at the staircase that led down to the basement. He barked.

"Good boy!" Charlie said, stroking the puppy's ears. "Maybe Bouncer went down there."

They hurried down the stairs. The basement was cool and still. Meg glanced around. Aside from an occasional ripple on the water's surface, nothing was moving.

"Where could Bouncer have gone?" she wondered.

Paco bounded down the stairs to join them. He sniffed at the water lilies on the edge of the pool. Then his paws pattered on the tiled floor as he sniffed at the creeping plant growing around the window. Suddenly, he gave a *yip* and his tail started to wag.

The twins grinned at each other. Could Paco have found Bouncer?

Charlie kneeled down and peered through the dense leaves. Meg crouched beside him. Just visible was a tiny, twitching pink nose, surrounded by long whiskers.

"Bouncer!" Charlie said.

CHAPTER 6

Moving slowly so he wouldn't startle Bouncer, Charlie reached into the plant and picked up the runaway rabbit. "Let's get you back upstairs," he said.

"Good job, Paco!" said Meg, tickling Paco's ears.

Saffron met them on the main floor, holding Bouncer's travel basket. "Here — put Bouncer in her basket and I'll take her up to her room," she said.

"Paco found Bouncer," said Meg. "He was amazing!"

The front door opened and Mom and Dad came in, carrying shopping bags. "We bought some extra rabbit food," Dad said.

Woof! Paco bounded toward them . . . and ran out the open door to Gazebo Square.

"Oh, no!" Charlie groaned. "We found Bouncer — but now we lost Paco!"

The twins ran out into the square, looking all around. The square was bustling with people whistling and singing as they set up their stalls.

"There he is!" exclaimed Meg, pointing.

Paco was sniffing at Juan's empty stall. The twins ran toward him, but the puppy took off into the crowd.

"Paco!" they yelled at the top of their lungs.

"Over there!" Charlie pointed to a yellow tail disappearing behind a crate of tomatoes. They dashed after Paco, but he'd already moved on.

"By the flower stall!" Meg cried. But by the time they got there, there was no puppy to be seen.

"He disappeared again," Charlie said with a groan. He ran his hands through his hair as he looked down the busy street. How could they find a puppy in all this commotion? And how could they tell Juan they'd lost him?

"Poor little Paco must be hungry again by now," Meg murmured. "Where would he go to find something to eat?"

The twins looked at each other.

"THE PET BAKERY!" they declared together.

Charlie thought hard, trying to remember what Juan had said when he told them about the bakery. Suddenly, he grinned. "It's on Park Street!"

They sprinted through Gazebo Square. On Park Street, they spotted the bakery's neon sign and went inside.

A man in a white apron was standing behind the counter.

"Hello," Meg said, trying to catch her breath. "Have you seen a yellow puppy?"

"You mean Paco?" the man replied.

"Yes! We're watching him for Juan," Charlie panted.

"I'm afraid I haven't seen him today." The baker picked up a tray labeled DOGGIE COOKIES and began to add the treats to the display on the counter. Then he stopped abruptly.

"That's odd," he noted, looking around. "Some of my cookies are missing. . . ."

"And I can hear chomping noises!" Meg said. She pointed to the beaded curtain at the back of the shop. "Back there!"

"That's the office," the baker said. He pulled the curtain aside — and revealed a yellow tail sticking out from behind a big metal filing cabinet.

"PACO!" Meg and Charlie called.

The fluffy tail thumped twice on the floor, then disappeared.

Slurp, slurp, chomp!

"Come out, you little rascal." The baker stuck his arm into the narrow space behind the filing cabinet. "I can't reach him," he sighed. He put his shoulder to the filing cabinet, but it didn't budge. "It's too heavy to move. We'll have to tempt him out with something. . . ."

"But Paco already has Doggie Cookies back there." Charlie groaned.

The baker scratched his head. "Is there anything else he likes?" he asked.

Meg and Charlie looked at each other.

"Yes!" they exclaimed together. The twins ran to the door.

"We'll be back soon!" Charlie called over his shoulder as he and Meg raced back to the hotel.

CHAPTER 7

Mom, Dad, and Saffron were in the kitchen when Charlie and Meg ran in.

Mom was holding the humane mouse-trap and looking at it with a puzzled frown. "I have no idea how the mouse got the cheese out of this," she muttered.

Saffron twisted the rings on her wrinkly fingers. "Some creatures can be very crafty," she observed with a grin.

"Like Paco!" Charlie said, turning to his great-great-aunt. "He stole some Doggie Cookies from the Pet Bakery, and now he doesn't want to leave. We need to borrow your feather boa to lure him out."

"Please," added Meg.

"Certainly, my dears." Saffron handed it to Meg. She winked. "My boa is having an awfully exciting time. I'm glad you came to stay!"

"Make sure you pay the baker for the cookies," Dad said, giving Charlie some money.

The twins hurried back to the bakery, the turquoise boa flapping behind them.

"Paco! Playtime!" Meg called when they reached the back room. She dangled the boa behind the filing cabinet.

There was a muffled *yap*. Meg bounced Saffron's boa up and down.

"*Yip!*" A second later, Paco backed out of his hidey-hole, a cookie in his mouth. Meg wriggled the boa along the ground in front of his nose. The puppy dropped the cookie and pounced on the turquoise feathers.

Charlie grabbed Paco's collar. "Got you!"

Paco spit out the boa and looked up innocently at the twins. He licked his lips.

"Better put him on a leash," the baker remarked, "just in case."

Meg and Charlie looked at each other in dismay. They'd forgotten to bring the leash!

Meg thought for a moment. "This will work," she said, looping the feather boa through Paco's collar. "You look awfully fancy now, Paco!"

Once Charlie had paid the baker, the twins led Paco back to the hotel.

Mom was at the reception desk, hanging up Saffron's old-fashioned red telephone.

"That was Juan," she told them. "His ankle is going to be okay. He's coming back this afternoon!"

Phew! Charlie and Meg grinned at each other. Juan was fine — and they'd found Paco just in time!

But Mom looked serious. "Dad and I need to come up with a plan to bring in more guests," she said. "Things here are worse than we thought. Saffron may have to sell Diamond Hotel and move into a home."

"No!" cried Charlie. "Saffron loves living on Gazebo Square — and so do we!"

～ ～ ～

"My friends, thank you so much!" Juan grinned as Paco leaped into his arms and licked his face.

The twins had met Juan at his stall the next morning. His ankle was in a cast, but he could stand with the help of a crutch.

"It was fun looking after Paco," Meg said. "We'll miss him."

Charlie sighed. "And we'll miss Gazebo Square if we have to leave," he whispered to Meg.

"Don't look so glum," Juan said. "Your mom and dad told me how well you cared for Paco, so I have a little surprise for you."

Juan put Paco on the ground and pulled a big cardboard box from beneath the table. Rustling noises were coming from inside.

Paco sniffed the box and wagged his tail happily.

The flaps of the box burst open. Two paws rested on the rim, and a football-sized ball of golden fluff looked up at them. It was a puppy! He tilted his head and blinked in the sunshine.

"Awww!" Meg said in delight. "He looks just like Paco, only smaller."

Juan lifted the puppy out of the box.

"This little guy's from the same litter as Paco," Juan explained. "He's the last one left, and he needs a good home."

"Do you think Mom and Dad will let us keep him?" Meg asked Charlie, hardly daring to believe their luck.

"I think they will." Juan laughed. "In fact, I already checked. He's all yours!"

CHAPTER 8

"Woof!" The new puppy wriggled in Juan's arms. Juan gently set him down on the pavement. The puppy ran around Paco, then rolled onto his back, kicking his legs in the air.

"He's *so* cute!" Meg tickled the puppy's warm, fuzzy tummy. "What should we call him?"

Charlie thought for a minute. "Buster," he said, "because of the way he busted out of the box!"

"Perfect." Meg giggled. "Do you think Buster likes Doggie Cookies as much as Paco does?"

At the sound of his name, Paco perked up his ears and thumped his tail.

"Paco had fun staying with you," Juan commented with a smile. "I'm off to visit my family in California soon. Do you think you could watch him while I'm away?"

Meg and Charlie looked at each other.

"We'd love to!" Meg declared.

"There's plenty of room at the hotel," Charlie added.

Just then, Carmen from the Cupcake Collection stall stopped by.

"Did I hear you say that Diamond Hotel is taking animal guests now?" she asked. "It would be so convenient if my Matilda could stay with you while I'm on vacation. . . ."

"Sounds like you're in business," Juan remarked, giving the twins a wink.

"We are!" Meg beamed at Charlie. "And I know just how we can save the hotel!"

➤ ═ ➤

Dad looked at his watch. "Five minutes before we reopen," he said. "That's just enough time for a final check!"

Meg and Charlie ran from room to room. It had been an incredibly busy two weeks! The hotel had been cleaned and painted from top to bottom, inside and out. The old furniture had been given to charity, and the carpets had been recycled and replaced with wooden floors or new rugs. Everyone had been working hard right up to the last minute.

Charlie threw open the door to the Egyptian room. "The guest room for cats!" he announced.

"Wow!" Meg gasped. The dingy old room looked fresh and clean, and the gold pharaoh statues sparkled. There were new kitty pens on either side of the old fireplace.

"I helped Mom paint the pens gold to match the pharaohs' crowns," Charlie said proudly. "And it was my idea to make the litter trays look like pyramids and the scratching posts like palm trees."

Meg peeked into a covered basket. There was a Ping-Pong ball and a catnip mouse on top of the fleecy blue cushion.

"Cats will love staying here," she said. "Come and see what Dad and I did." Meg pulled Charlie to the other end of the hallway and flung open the door to the forest room.

In each corner was a big triangular pen painted green, with its own water bowl and basket. The baskets all had comfy cushions and ball-on-a-rope doggie toys inside.

"Dogs will definitely feel right at home here," Charlie said, laughing and looking

at the plastic lamppost in the middle of the room.

"Did you check the small pets' room?" Mom called up the stairs.

"On our way!" Charlie and Meg ran up to the top floor of the hotel and opened the door of the old playroom. It had been dirty and abandoned when they'd first arrived. But now the walls and the floor were painted a fresh, grassy green, spotted with white daisies. At one end were hutches for rabbits or guinea pigs. Each hutch had its own run, with real grass and a wooden trough planted with dandelions, lettuce, and carrots!

"Saffron did an amazing job in here!" Meg said.

"Is everything ready?" Dad called.

"Yes!" Meg and Charlie exclaimed, hurtling down the stairs to the reception area. Saffron, Mom, Dad, and Buster were waiting for them.

Saffron straightened the frame of the new certificate for boarding animals that was mounted on the wall. "My dears, you have given me a new lease on life," she said happily.

With that, Dad opened the sky-blue front door and they all stepped outside.

The sound of clapping drowned out the noise of the men working on the old archway. Charlie and Meg beamed with pride. All of the market vendors were gathered around the entrance to the hotel! Juan gave them a cheery wave. He had a hand drum tucked under his arm, and Paco was sitting by his side.

The twins each took hold of a corner of the scarf they'd draped over the new hotel sign. It was one of Saffron's scarves, covered in swirls of neon orange, purple, and green.

Juan began a drumroll.

Ta-da!

Charlie and Meg pulled the scarf away from the new sign. It read:

PET HOTEL

Saffron waved her feather boa in the air, and the crowd cheered.

"Woof, woof, woof!" Paco and Buster wagged their tails.

Over in the gazebo, a band struck up a joyful tune.

Meg and Charlie clapped their hands and joined in the dancing. They couldn't wait to welcome more guests to Gazebo Square's brand-new Pet Hotel!

Check out who's checking in —
don't miss the next Pet Hotel book!

Pet Hotel #2: A Big Surprise

CHAPTER 1

As the sun rose higher in the sky, Gazebo Square echoed with cheerful cries of "Good morning!"

People behind the booths were setting out their brightly colored displays as they greeted their first customers of the day. The square was buzzing with happy chatter, and the air smelled like coffee and freshly baked cinnamon buns. Over at the gazebo bandstand, three boys were playing a happy tune.

"Good morning!" eight-year-old twins Meg and Charlie shouted to their friends as they hurried past. Charlie's backpack was full of yummy breakfast treats. Meg was clutching the handle of a big straw basket in one hand and a dog leash in the other. At the end of the leash was a fluffy golden puppy with a brown marking around one eye, like a pirate's eye patch. Meg smiled proudly. Buster looked so cute prancing along on his big puppy paws.

"Woof!" Buster suddenly barked and tugged his leash out of Meg's hand.

"He spotted his brother!" Charlie said with a laugh. He pointed to another ball of golden fur, shooting out from under the Cocina Mexicana stall, which was run by their friend Juan. Juan's puppy, Paco, was wagging his tail so hard that it was a blur.

"Woof! Woof! Woof!" The two puppies pounced gleefully on each other and rolled over and over, toppling a sack of sweet potatoes.

"Oops!" Meg murmured. She untangled Buster's leash and picked up the potatoes.

"Oh, that's no problem," said Juan. His face lit up in a huge grin. "I love to see Paco play with Buster. I played with my brother like that when we were small, too!"

Meg and Charlie giggled.

"Buster looks great," Juan went on. "I guess he likes living with you at Pet Hotel."

"He loves it!" Meg said happily.

"Buster gets along with all the guests," Charlie said. "Even the cats!"

"That's good to hear," Juan said, unpacking a box of pineapples. "Have a great day, you two. Thanks for stopping by!"

"See you later," Meg and Charlie called, waving good-bye. They walked across the street to a tall old brownstone with a freshly painted front door. Above the door was a big new sign that read PET HOTEL.

Meg and Charlie both looked up at the sign and beamed from ear to ear. When they'd first arrived in Gazebo Square, their great-great-aunt Saffron's hotel had been a regular hotel for people, but it was so run-down that it didn't have any guests. When Juan had hurt his ankle, Meg and Charlie had taken care of Paco — and realized that the hotel made a perfect place for pets to stay. It was already an amazing success! Right now, their guests were six goldfish, two cats, three dogs, a rabbit, four guinea pigs, and a —

"Wheeeeep!" An ear-piercing screech came from inside the hotel, making Charlie, Meg, and Buster leap into the air.

Meg held tightly to Buster's leash and carefully pushed open the sky-blue door.

"Wheee-wheee-wheeep!" The noise was coming from upstairs.

Charlie shut the hotel door firmly behind them so that none of the pets could get out.

There was another screech, as loud as a train coming into a station.

Meg giggled as she hung Buster's leash on a peg inside the front door. "Any second now, the singing will start," she said.

Charlie quickly clapped his hands over his ears.

Sure enough, a voice screeched down the stairs: *"You ain't nothing but a hound dog! You ain't nothing but a hound dog!"* It sounded like an opera singer being strangled.

Buster threw back his head. *"Aooo-ooo!"* he howled.

"Elvis is awake," Meg said, giggling. She and Charlie dropped their shopping bags on the reception desk and raced upstairs to see their latest guest.

WHERE EVERY PUPPY FINDS A HOME

KITTY CORNER

Where kitties get the love they need

These purr-fect kittens need a home!